Love Poetry & Pictures

Volume 1

Love Poetry & Pictures

Volume 1

Satirical Media

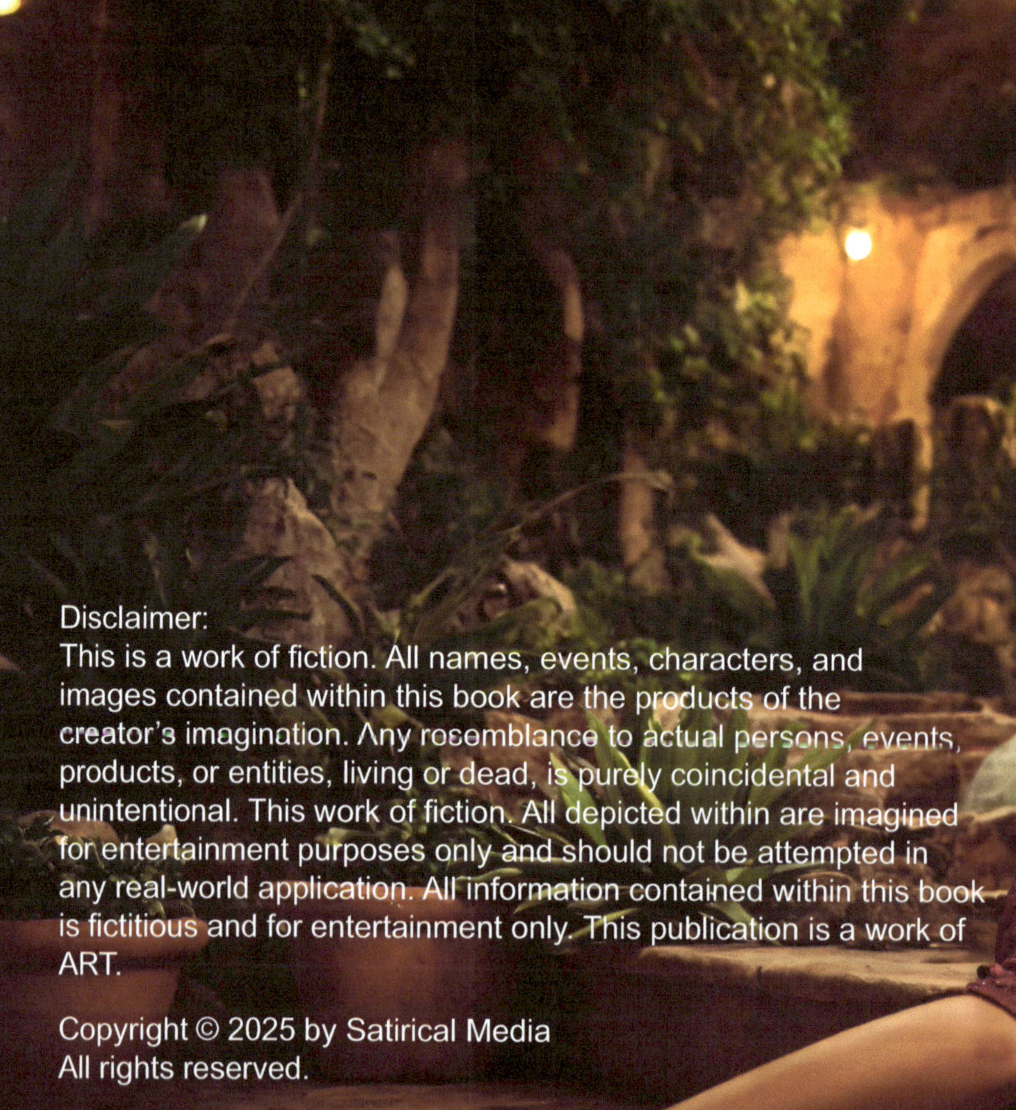

ISBN: 978-1-923365-03-2

"To Lovers Everywhere"

Table of Contents

'Better to have loved and lost than never to have loved at all'

Alfred, Lord Tennyson (1809-92)

The Spark

Poems about

the thrilling first

moments of love.

Whispered Promises

In the hush of twilight's glow,

Your heartbeat speaks what words don't know.

A promise lingers in your gaze,

A quiet vow that time won't raze.

Your hand in mine, our world fades out,

In love like this, there is no doubt.

A whispered promise, soft and true.

Forever starts with me and you.

A Chance Encounter
A brush of hands, a fleeting smile,
A connection formed in just a while.
The world around fades to gray,
As your laugh lights up my day.

Unspoken

Words were lost, but something grew,
A feeling strong, a thrill so new.
Eyes that linger, hearts that race,
A spark ignites in this shared space.

The First Hello
Your voice, a melody, soft and sweet,
My heart skips with every beat.
One "hello" and everything's changed,
A destiny now rearranged.

Unexpected Flame
I didn't know your name or face,
But felt a warmth I can't replace.
A stranger once, but now I see,
A spark that's bound to set me free.

Eternal Seconds

A single second stretched so long,
My world's new rhythm, your love's song.
In one brief glance, I felt it all,
The start of a love I can't forestall.

Coffee Shop Magic
A spilled latte, a shared smile,
Your presence made the mishap worthwhile.
A spark over cappuccinos and cream,
Was this chance, or just a dream?

First Glance
Across the room, our eyes collide,
A quiet pull, I can't hide.
The air electric, the world stands still,
My heart races, against my will.
Dr. Love
Passion Hospital

Morning Rush
In a crowded train, I found your gaze,
A quiet magic amidst the haze.
The rush of morning, yet time stood still,
As I felt my heart bend to your will.

The Stranger's Smile
A smile exchanged, no words were said,
Yet thoughts of you now fill my head.
What brought you here, what brought you near?
A spark so bright, it's crystal clear.

The Elevator Pause

Two floors up, but an eternity,

A spark that danced between you and me.

The air grew thick, the silence loud,

Two hearts connected within the crowd.

Library Whispers
In quiet corners, our eyes first met,
A story begun I won't forget.
Your glance a bookmark in my heart,
The prologue to our romantic start.

Rainy Day Spark
Beneath one umbrella, close and tight,
A rainy day turned pure delight.
Your laughter warmed the coldest rain,
And left me longing to see you again.

Cinematic Chance
Seats apart in a dim-lit show,
Your silhouette bathed in the screen's glow.
The plot forgot, I only see,
The spark of love awakening in me.

Flames
and
Longing
Sensual and
passionate verses.

Your Skin, My Symphony
Your touch is music, your scent a song,
I've craved your rhythm all along.
Each sigh, a note, each kiss, a chord,
Together, a masterpiece we've explored.

Gravity

I'm drawn to you, a magnetic force,
A tidal wave changing my course.
Each touch, a pull, each sigh, a fall,
Lost in your gravity, I want it all.

Burning Midnight

Beneath the stars, we shed our fears,
Whispered truths and silent tears.
Your touch ignites a wild desire,
My heart consumed by midnight's fire.

Red Silk
Draped in red silk, your gaze holds mine,
A sensual story told line by line.
Each whisper, a shiver, each look, a plea,
A love as deep as the endless sea.

Velvet Heat

Your skin, a canvas of velvet heat,
Each kiss a story, our passion complete.
In your embrace, I'm free to fall,
A prisoner to the thrill of it all.

Crimson Sheets

Tangled in crimson, our secrets unfold,
A love so hot, it burns through the cold.
Your hands are flames, your breath a plea,
You've set my soul eternally free.

Candle Glow

In candlelight, your shadow plays,
A siren song that pulls and sways.
The wax melts slow, the fire persists,
Just like the heat of your tempting kiss.

Pulse

I feel your pulse beneath my hand,
A rhythm only we understand.
A fevered dance, a sacred space,
Lost in the heat of your embrace.

Edge of Breath

Your lips linger just out of reach,
A lesson only longing can teach.
The air between us, electric and tight,
A fire that burns through the night.

Flame to Ash
We burn together, fierce and bright,
A fleeting dance in the pale moonlight.
Even as ashes begin to form,
I crave the passion of your storm.

Eclipse

You eclipse my thoughts, a blazing sun,
A firestorm that can't be outrun.
Your passion blinds, your love consumes,
I'm lost in you, in your endless blooms.

Wildfire

One spark, and now I'm ablaze,

Your love, a wildfire, an endless craze.

I'd let it burn, consume me whole,

If only to keep your heart's control.

Wine-Stained Nights
Lips stained red, your taste lingers sweet,
A heady rush, a lover's treat.
In every sip, I find your fire,
A vintage aged to fuel desire.

Heartache and Healing

Exploring the bittersweet moments of love.

Empty Spaces

I keep your voice in a secret drawer,

Replay it when I can't take more.

The spaces you've left, they whisper your name,

Yet somehow, I'm stronger all the same.

Fractured Reflections

In the mirror, I see your ghost,
The love I gave, what I wanted most.
A cracked reflection, a broken frame,
Yet I rise, reborn from the pain.

Shadows Fade

Your shadow lingered, a haunting trace,
But time has softened your fleeting face.
Each day, the ache becomes less clear,
Healing grows where there was fear.

Ashes of Us

From the ashes of us, I'll build anew,
A life not shaped by loving you.
The fire's gone, but I still stand,
Stronger now, with open hands.

Unspoken Goodbyes

The words we never dared to say,
Are heavy stones along my way.
But silence heals what words could not,
And I find peace in the battles we fought.

Rain Soaked Letters

I read your letters in the rain,
Each word a drop, each line a stain.
Washed clean now, their weight erased,
A freedom found, a love displaced.

Wounds and Wings

You broke me open, left me raw,

But from those wounds, I grew a claw.

A bird that soars, no cage, no ties,

Free to conquer boundless skies.

The Ache of Almost
We were almost, but not quite there,
A love that hung in the fragile air.
Yet "almost" taught me what I need,
A love that stays, a heart that bleeds.

Echoes

Your voice still echoes through my mind,
A melody that's left behind.
But with each note, the sound grows dim,
A fading trace of what has been.

Closure's Kiss

One last kiss, a final sigh,
We said goodbye, we learned to fly.
What once was "us" is now just me,
But oh, how sweet the memory.

Threadbare Love
Our love unravelled, thread by thread,
But in those fibres, hope was bred.
I sew my future, stitch by stitch,
With lessons learned and a heart that's rich.

Falling Upward
You left me falling, but I found the ground,
A place where strength and peace abound.
Now I rise, no longer lost,
A love rebuilt, despite the cost.

Forever Ours
Celebrating
enduring love
and connection.

Timeless Together
Your laugh still echoes through my years,
A melody that calms my fears.
With every wrinkle, every line,
I see the proof: you are mine.

Evergreen
Seasons shift, and so do we,
Yet love remains, like an evergreen tree.
Rooted deep, we'll never part,
Bound forever, heart to heart.

The Quiet We

It's in the silence where we shine,

Your hand in mine, the stars align.

No need for words, no need for show,

It's in your presence I truly know.

Morning Light
The sun rises, soft and slow,
Casting warmth in your golden glow.
Every day begins with you,
My forever, my dream come true.

Soul Threads
Woven tight, our souls entwine,
A tapestry of love divine.
Each thread a promise, strong and true,
A masterpiece created by me and you.

Golden Years
In silver hair and stories told,
In hands that never lose their hold,
We find a love that never fades,
A legacy our hearts have made.

Eternal Flame
Our fire burns steady, year by year,
A guiding light that draws us near.
Through every storm, through joy and pain,
You are my shelter, my heart's refrain.

Horizon
As the horizon meets the sea,
That's how your love feels to me.
Endless, boundless, forever in view,
A perfect line of me and you.

Promise

In every vow, in every glance,
In every fleeting circumstance,
I promise now, I'll promise then,
To love you time and time again.

Home

Your arms are where I find my rest,
The place where life feels most blessed.
No house, no walls, no grand design,
Just you, my love—forever mine.

Boundless
Not even time can wear us thin,
Our love is boundless, deep within.
A force that grows as years go by,
My every day, my sweetest why.

After the Rain
Through tempests fierce and skies turned gray,
We've found our rainbow on display.
The storm has passed, the skies are clear,
Forever starts with you right here.

The End

www.ingramcontent.com/pod-product-compliance
Lightning Source LLC
Chambersburg PA
CBHW041407010726
47507CB00001B/31